# THE JEDI
# AND THE FORCE

## The Jedi & The Force

**Managing Editor** Laura Gilbert
**Design Manager** Maxine Pedliham
**Art Director** Lisa Lanzarini
**Publisher** Julie Ferris
**Publishing Director** Simon Beecroft
**Senior DTP Designer** David McDonald
**Creative Manager** Sarah Harland
**Senior Producer** Alex Bell

### Reading Consultant
Dr. Linda Gambrell, PhD

### Lucasfilm Ltd.
**Executive Editor** Jonathan W. Rinzler
**Art Director** Troy Alders
**Story Group** Rayne Roberts, Pablo Hidalgo, Leland Chee

**Editorial Assistant** Lauren Nesworthy

This edition published in the United States in 2015 by
DK Publishing
345 Hudson Street
New York, New York 10014
A Penguin Random House Company

First published as three separate titles: Star Wars: Obi-Wan Kenobi, Jedi Knight (2012),
Star Wars: The Story of Darth Vader (2008), Star Wars: The Legendary Yoda (2013)

002–271025–Jun/14

A catalog record for this book is available
from the Library of Congress.

ISBN 978-1-4351-5416-2

Printed and bound by L.Rex Printing Co., Ltd, China

www.starwars.com
www.dk.com

A WORLD OF IDEAS:
**SEE ALL THERE IS TO KNOW**

# THE JEDI
# AND THE FORCE

# Contents

Obi-Wan Kenobi Jedi Knight .............. 5

The Story of Darth Vader ................... 51

The Legendary Yoda .......................... 97

Glossary................................................. 142

Index ..................................................... 143

## STAR WARS ®

### OBI-WAN KENOBI
# JEDI KNIGHT

Written by Catherine Saunders

# Legendary Jedi

Meet Obi-Wan Kenobi, a brave Jedi Knight. He went on many missions and fought in many battles to keep the galaxy safe and peaceful.

Obi-Wan Kenobi was born on the planet Stewjon and lived there with his parents and his brother Owen. Young Obi-Wan began to show signs that he had Jedi powers, so he left his family to live on Coruscant. There, Obi-Wan became a youngling and was trained in the ways of the Jedi by Master Yoda.

The best younglings eventually become apprentices, or Padawans, to Jedi Knights. Obi-Wan showed promise, but he was not chosen to be a Padawan.

# Padawan training

While many of his friends became Padawans, Obi-Wan Kenobi was sent to work in a mining colony on the Outer Rim of the galaxy. He believed his dream of becoming a Jedi Knight was over, until Jedi Master Qui-Gon Jinn finally spotted his potential. Qui-Gon chose Obi-Wan to be his apprentice and Obi-Wan's life as a Jedi began. As a Padawan, Obi-Wan accompanied Qui-Gon on missions all over the galaxy.

*Obi-Wan in his Padawan robes.*

*The young apprentice learns many things from his powerful Master.*

Obi-Wan learned how to use Jedi wisdom, diplomacy, and negotiation to settle disputes, but he also learned how to use his Force powers and combat skills. As the years passed, Obi-Wan's Jedi powers grew stronger and he hoped to be given the chance to face the Jedi Trials. If he passed the Trials, he would finally become a Jedi Knight.

# An important mission

A trade dispute gave Obi-Wan the chance to prove himself. The Trade Federation blockaded the planet of Naboo and the galaxy was on the brink of war. Obi-Wan and Qui-Gon helped Queen Amidala of Naboo to escape the blockade. They all set off for Coruscant to seek help.

*Qui-Gon and Obi-Wan voyaged through the planet core with Jar Jar Binks on their way to the city of Theed.*

Unfortunately, the Jedi's ship was damaged by the blockade and they were forced to land on the desert planet of Tatooine for repairs. Here they encountered a mysterious Sith.

Eventually, the Jedi and their passengers made it to Coruscant. The Jedi Council decided that Obi-Wan and Qui-Gon should go back to Naboo and help the Queen defeat the Trade Federation.

*On Tatooine, a deadly Sith Lord pursued the Queen of Naboo.*

# Sith duel

Sith Lord Darth Maul tried to destroy the Jedi on Tatooine. While the Queen and her troops fought the Trade Federation, Obi-Wan Kenobi and Qui-Gon Jinn took on the powerful Sith inside the city's power generator. It was a tough battle. Maul soon separated the Jedi Master from his Padawan and Obi-Wan could only watch as the Sith killed Qui-Gon.

**Sith**
The Jedi want peace and justice, but the Sith want power. The Jedi believed that they had destroyed their old enemies 1,000 years ago, but they were wrong.

*Obi-Wan gained strength and courage from the light side of the Force.*

It was time for the young Padawan to prove himself. Although he fought bravely, Maul was able to push Obi-Wan into the generator's core. Luckily, Obi-Wan Kenobi was smarter than Maul. He used the Force to snatch Qui-Gon's lightsaber and jump up and defeat the Sith.

# Jedi Knight

The Jedi Council decided that Obi-Wan had proved himself worthy of the title "Jedi Knight" by defeating Maul—he did not need to face the Jedi Trials. Now, as a Jedi Knight, Obi-Wan Kenobi needed an apprentice. Keeping a promise he made to Qui-Gon, Obi-Wan chose Anakin Skywalker as his Padawan.

*The apprentice had become the teacher. Obi-Wan tried to teach Anakin how to be a good Jedi.*

**Master Yoda**

Grand Master Yoda was the wisest and most powerful Jedi. He sensed that Anakin Skywalker had much fear and anger in him and did not think he should be trained as a Jedi.

Over the next few years, Obi-Wan took his young Padawan on many missions and tried to teach him the ways of the Force. The Jedi and Padawan developed a close friendship. At times, Obi-Wan wished Anakin would be more cautious, but he believed Anakin was destined to become a great Jedi in the future.

# Dangerous mission

Obi-Wan and Anakin were given the job of protecting their old friend, Padmé Amidala. The former Queen of Naboo was now a senator in the Galactic Republic, but someone was trying to kill her. When an assassin made an attempt on Padmé's life, the Jedi leapt into action to save her.

*Obi-Wan and Anakin were determined to find out who wanted to kill senator Amidala.*

**Forbidden love**

Anakin Skywalker was in love with Padmé, but Jedi are not supposed to form emotional attachments. Padmé felt the same about Anakin so they hid their feelings from Obi-Wan.

Using their piloting and tracking skills, Obi-Wan and his Padawan chased the assassin, Zam Wesell, but she was killed by a poisonous dart before they could find out who she was working for. Obi-Wan examined the poisonous dart for clues. He ordered Anakin to stay and protect Padmé, while he went off in search of more information.

# Clever Jedi

Obi-Wan was determined to find out who wanted to kill Senator Amidala. He learned that the dart came from the planet of Kamino, an aquatic planet located beyond the Outer Rim of the galaxy. When Obi-Wan visited the planet, he received a warm welcome from the Kaminoans. However, he was shocked to learn that they were building a huge clone army, apparently on the orders of deceased Jedi Master, Sifo-Dyas.

**Clones**
Each clone soldier was genetically identical which means they looked the same. They were bred to follow orders.

Obi-Wan also met Jango Fett, a Mandalorian bounty hunter whose genetic code had been used to make all the clones. The Jedi Council ordered Obi-Wan to bring Jango Fett to Coruscant for questioning. But, the bounty hunter was not prepared to come voluntarily....

# Bounty hunter duel

*Boba Fett*

Jango Fett and his son Boba tried to flee, but Obi-Wan caught up with them before they could board their ship, *Slave I*. The Jedi and the bounty hunter fought a fierce duel. To make matters worse for Obi-Wan, young Boba started firing at him from *Slave I*. Finally, the Jedi realized this was one battle he could not win.

The bounty hunter escaped, but the wise Jedi attached a tracking device to Fett's ship. Obi-Wan followed the bounty hunter to a planet named Geonosis, but even more trouble awaited him there....

# An enemy revealed

Obi-Wan was close to uncovering something very big. On Geonosis, he learned that a group of Separatists was plotting to break away from the Republic. They were led by the former Jedi, Count Dooku. Obi-Wan discovered that Dooku had been behind the attempts to kill Padmé and that Dooku and his allies were building a massive droid army. Obi-Wan told the Jedi Council what he had found out before he was captured by Dooku.

**Count Dooku**
Count Dooku had turned to the dark side and become a Sith Lord. His Sith name was Darth Tyranus.

Dooku tried to convince Obi-Wan to join his army, but the Jedi was not tempted by power. Anakin and Padmé arrived on Geonosis to help Obi-Wan, but they were captured too. Obi-Wan, Anakin, and Padmé were sentenced to death and led to a huge arena to await their fate.

*Dooku told Obi-Wan that the Senate was secretly being controlled by a Sith Lord, but Obi-Wan did not believe him.*

# The Battle of Geonosis

Obi-Wan, Anakin, and Padmé discovered their executioners were three huge creatures—a nexu, a reek, and an acklay. The Jedi and the Senator fought off the beasts, but Dooku sent in droidekas to kill them. Just when it seemed that all was lost, 200 Jedi fighters joined the battle.

Unfortunately, Dooku had been expecting the Jedi and deployed his droid army. The Jedi Knights were outnumbered, until Master Yoda arrived with the huge clone army. The Battle of Geonosis had begun! Dooku used the opportunity to escape, but Obi-Wan was not about to let the Sith go....

*In the arena battle on Geonosis, the Jedi were aided by Master Mace Windu.*

# Jedi duel

*Dooku used deadly Force lightning on Anakin.*

Obi-Wan and Anakin caught up with Dooku, and prepared to do battle with him. Obi-Wan wanted them to attack him together, but Anakin rushed ahead. Dooku quickly wounded the impulsive Padawan, leaving Obi-Wan to duel him alone.

*Obi-Wan struggled against Dooku's dark side powers.*

*Faced with the choice of defeating the Sith or saving the Jedi, Master Yoda was forced to let Dooku escape.*

The Jedi fought bravely, but Dooku soon had him at his mercy. He was about to deliver a fatal blow, when Anakin regained consciousness and saved his Master.

Obi-Wan had taught his apprentice well, but the Sith was too strong for him and severed Anakin's hand. Once again, only the timely arrival of Yoda saved the two Jedi.

# The Clone Wars

The events on Geonosis were the
start of the Clone Wars. The clone
army, now called the Grand Army
of the Republic, fought many battles
against the Separatist Droid Army.
During that time the Jedi became
generals, rather than peacekeepers.
Obi-Wan Kenobi became a great
leader, and fought many battles
alongside his apprentice Anakin.

Commander Cody was a brave
clone trooper and a good friend
to Obi-Wan Kenobi.

The Clone Wars continued
for three years, and Obi-Wan
Kenobi's reputation grew.
He was a brave general and
skilful fighter, but Obi-Wan
was also famous for his desire to
find diplomatic solutions. In fact,
he was nicknamed "The
Negotiator" because he always
hoped to find a peaceful
outcome to any dispute.

Obi-Wan attained the
rank of Jedi Master
and was invited to
become a member
of the Jedi Council.

# The Battle of Coruscant

Obi-Wan and Anakin were sent on a mission to rescue Chancellor Palpatine, who had been kidnapped by Dooku and Separatist leader General Grievous.

For a second time, the Jedi faced Count Dooku in a duel. However, this time the Sith overpowered Obi-Wan using a Force choke. Anakin had to fight Dooku alone.

Encouraged by
Palpatine, Anakin
murdered a
defenseless Dooku—
a violation of the Jedi
Code. Palpatine also

*Dooku was betrayed by
Chancellor Palpatine.*

wanted Anakin to leave Obi-Wan
to die, but the Jedi refused. When
Obi-Wan regained consciousness,
he sensed that he had missed
something important.

*With R2-D2's help, Anakin crash-landed the* Invisible Hand *after it split in two.*

# Jedi wisdom

Obi-Wan was growing deeply suspicious of Chancellor Palpatine. He saw that he was becoming very powerful and Obi-Wan did not trust him. Obi-Wan was also concerned for his former Padwan, Anakin. Obi-Wan tried to talk to him, but the troubled Jedi would not listen.

*Obi-Wan was worried that Anakin was more influenced by the politician than the Jedi Council.*

Unfortunately, Obi-Wan was called away on a mission to find General Grievous. Without Obi-Wan around to guide him, Anakin listened more and more to Palpatine. Finally, Palpatine revealed his secret identity to Anakin. He offered the Jedi great power and urged him to turn to the dark side. Anakin agreed, taking on a secret Sith identity—Darth Vader.

*Obi-Wan felt deeply troubled.*

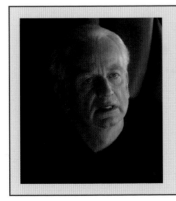

**Chancellor Palpatine**
Palpatine was the leader of the Senate but he had a secret—he was really a Sith Lord, Darth Sidious. And he was plotting to take over the galaxy.

# Cyborg duel

General Grievous was a powerful Separatist leader. Obi-Wan tracked him to the planet of Utapau and faced him in a duel. The Jedi had only one lightsaber, but the General wielded four. Obi-Wan sliced off two of the cyborg's hands to even the odds.

Eventually the Jedi Master killed Grievous by shooting him with the cyborg's own blaster. With Grievous dead, Obi-Wan's mission on Utapau was complete and the Clone Wars were finally over. However, back on Coruscant things were about to get very bad indeed....

# The Jedi purge

While Obi-Wan was on Utapau, Chancellor Palpatine issued Order 66 and the Clone Army turned against the Jedi. Obi-Wan survived an attack by his clone troopers, but when he returned to Coruscant he learned that the Sith Darth Vader had killed all the Jedi in the Jedi Temple.

*Few Jedi survived Order 66.*

Obi-Wan realized that things were worse than he ever imagined— Palpatine was a Sith Lord and Vader was his former Padawan, Anakin. Obi-Wan had no choice— he would have to fight his best friend.

# Epic duel

Obi-Wan tracked his former friend to the planet Mustafar. Full of anger, Vader attacked Obi-Wan. The Jedi Master was a legendary fighter, but so was Anakin, and now he had the power of the dark side of the Force.

*This was one of the greatest duels in the history of the galaxy, and one of the most important.*

**A new enemy**
Darth Vader did not die. Palpatine rescued him and had him re-built, using black armor to protect his body and a helmet to help him breathe.

The former friends fought hard, each determined to win. However, Anakin had grown arrogant and it proved to be his downfall. As the Sith made a daring leap at Obi-Wan, the Jedi Master was able to strike him with his lightsaber. Obi-Wan finally had Anakin at his mercy. But the Jedi Master was unwilling to kill a defenseless man. Instead, Obi-Wan chose to let the Force decide Darth Vader's fate.

# Into hiding

With the galaxy in turmoil and
the Jedi in danger, Obi-Wan turned
his attention to Anakin's wife,
Padmé. The Senator was pregnant,
so Obi-Wan took her to a safe place
to give birth. Obi-Wan knew that
her children would be in danger if
Palpatine learned of their existence,
so he came up with a plan.

*Padmé gave birth to twins—a boy and a girl. But she had no
desire to live without Anakin.*

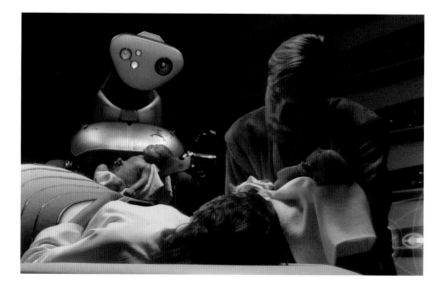

*Anakin's stepbrother, Owen, and his wife, Beru, raised Luke Skywalker on Tatooine.*

He gave the girl, Leia, to Senator Organa from the planet Alderaan and she was raised as a princess. Obi-Wan took the boy, Luke, to Tatooine. Once he was sure that Anakin's children were safe, Obi-Wan Kenobi went into hiding.

*With Palpatine now controlling the galaxy, it was no longer safe to be a Jedi.*

# Ben Kenobi

Obi-Wan remained on Tatooine where he could check on Luke from a distance. He called himself "Ben" Kenobi and lived a quiet life, keeping his Jedi powers a secret. During that time, the evil Sith Lord Sidious built a powerful Empire. He ruled the galaxy with Darth Vader. Everyone lived in fear of the Emperor, only the Rebel Alliance dared to oppose him.

*Obi-Wan decided that the time was right to give Luke his father's lightsaber.*

*Obi-Wan also offered to begin teaching Luke in the ways of the Force.*

One day, Luke was attacked by a Tusken Raider while searching for his new droid, R2-D2. Obi-Wan rescued Luke and immediately saw his Jedi potential. He invited Luke to go on a mission, but he refused. Eventually, Luke changed his mind. It was time for Obi-Wan to become a Jedi once more.

### R2-D2

R2-D2 had a message from the Rebel leader, Princess Leia, for Obi-Wan. He had the plans for the Emperor's Death Star and Leia wanted Obi-Wan to deliver them to her father on Alderaan.

# Important mission

Obi-Wan needed to deliver Princess Leia's message. He hired a smuggler named Han Solo, his Wookiee co-pilot, Chewbacca, and their ship the *Millennium Falcon*.

Before they could reach Alderaan, it was destroyed by the Death Star.

*C-3PO and R2-D2 played holochess against Chewbacca on the Millennium Falcon. Han advised them to let the Wookiee win.*

Worse still, the *Millennium Falcon* was also captured by the

Death Star. As Obi-Wan tried to disable the Death Star's tractor beam so the *Millennium Falcon* could escape, he met his old friend Darth Vader.

# Final duel

Obi-Wan was not surprised to see Vader. In fact, he had been expecting him. Obi-Wan knew exactly what he needed to do to help Luke, Leia, and Han escape. He ignited his lightsaber and prepared to duel.

Vader was happy to duel his former Master, but this time he was determined to win. As the wise old Jedi and the terrifying Sith fought, Vader mocked Obi-Wan. However, as soon as Obi-Wan knew that Luke, Han and Leia were safe, he extinguished his lightsaber and summoned the Force. Seconds before Vader would have struck a fatal blow, Obi-Wan disappeared. The Jedi had left his physical body behind but he would live on as part of the Force.

# Guiding light

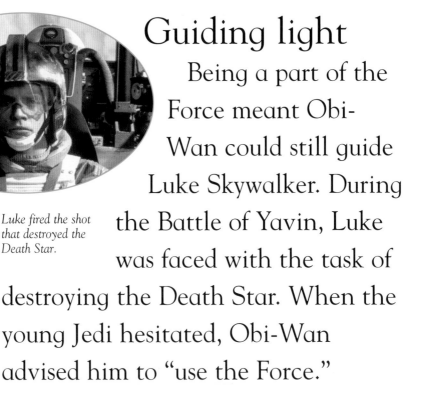

*Luke fired the shot that destroyed the Death Star.*

Being a part of the Force meant Obi-Wan could still guide Luke Skywalker. During the Battle of Yavin, Luke was faced with the task of destroying the Death Star. When the young Jedi hesitated, Obi-Wan advised him to "use the Force."

*When Luke learned that his father was Darth Vader, Obi-Wan helped him to control his emotions and revealed that he also had a twin sister—Leia.*

*Only the greatest Jedi such as Anakin Skywalker, Yoda, and Obi-Wan Kenobi have the power to become a part of the living Force.*

Later, he told Luke to seek out Yoda in the Dagobah system and persuaded the old Jedi to train him.

Obi-Wan Kenobi was one of the greatest Jedi who ever lived. He went on many missions and fought in many battles to keep the galaxy safe. Now he is one with the Force, joined by Yoda and Anakin as they watch over future generations.

# THE STORY OF
# DARTH VADER

Written by
Catherine Saunders

# The Story of Darth Vader

Take a look at Darth Vader—if you dare! He is a very dangerous man with many terrifying powers. Darth Vader is a ruthless Sith Lord who helps rule the galaxy for the evil Emperor Palpatine.

But Darth Vader was not always the masked Sith you see now. Once he was a talented Jedi Knight named Anakin Skywalker. Read on and uncover the story of how a promising young Jedi turned to the dark side of the Force.

**Emperor Palpatine**
From the first moment he met Anakin Skywalker, Palpatine knew that he could be the perfect apprentice.

# Young Anakin Skywalker

Anakin Skywalker grew up a slave on the desert planet Tatooine. His mother Shmi could not explain how Anakin came to be born—he had no father.

Anakin was a gentle child and he loved his mother very much. From a young age he was skilled at making and fixing mechanical things. When he was nine years old he built a droid named C-3P0 to help his mother. However, Anakin was impulsive and liked to take risks.

**Slave owner**
Anakin and Shmi were owned by a junk dealer named Watto and had to do whatever he told them. Watto made them work very hard.

# A Special Calling

When Jedi Qui-Gon Jinn and Obi-Wan Kenobi landed on Tatooine to repair their damaged ship, they met Anakin Skywalker. Qui-Gon realized the young slave had the potential to be a great Jedi.

*Qui-Gon checked Anakin's blood to see if he had Force powers. He certainly did!*

When Anakin offered to enter a
dangerous Podrace, Qui-Gon seized the
opportunity to win the parts he needed
for his ship and Anakin's freedom. The
Jedi was sure that Anakin's Force powers
would help him to win the race. He was
right. Freed from slavery, Anakin was
able to leave Tatooine with the Jedi, but
first he had to say goodbye to his mother.

*Anakin was happy to be embarking on a new adventure, but he missed his mother very much.*

# A New Life Begins

After leaving Tatooine, Qui-Gon asked the Jedi Council to let Anakin become his apprentice, but it refused. The Council thought that Anakin was already too old, and some wise members also sensed danger in Anakin's future.

So, when Qui-Gon and Obi-Wan went on a special mission, Anakin went too.

**Padmé Amidala**
Queen Padmé Amidala of
Naboo was only a few years
older than Anakin and the
young boy developed strong
feelings for her.

Anakin and the Jedi liberated the
planet Naboo from the Trade Federation
invasion. When Anakin piloted a
starfighter and destroyed the Trade
Federation's Droid Control Ship, the Jedi
Council changed its mind. Although Qui-
Gon had been killed by a Sith, Obi-Wan
promised to train Anakin instead.

# Jedi Training

Anakin Skywalker returned to the Jedi Temple on the capital planet Coruscant to begin his training. He was taught how to use and control his incredible Force powers. Anakin was also instructed in the ways of the Jedi Knights. Jedi must be calm and not governed by emotions. They are peace-loving and use their skills only to defend, never to attack.

As Jedi Master Obi-Wan Kenobi's Padawan learner or apprentice, Anakin came to view Obi-Wan as the closest thing he had to a father figure.

**The Force**
The energy known as the Force is everywhere. Jedi learn to use the light side of the Force for good, while their enemies, the Sith, use the dark side for greed and power.

# Increasing Frustration

Anakin loved and respected Obi-Wan, but often felt frustrated by him. Anakin was confident in his Jedi abilities, and felt that Obi-Wan was holding him back. He was tired of being just a Padawan.

Obi-Wan knew that Anakin had the potential to be a powerful Jedi Knight.

But he also believed that Anakin had not yet mastered his emotions, as a Jedi should. Obi-Wan was proved right when Anakin was reunited with Padmé Amidala after ten years. The feelings that Anakin had felt for her as a boy had not gone away. Soon he would no longer be able to control them.

# Powerful Friend

The galaxy was formed as a Republic, which meant that it was ruled by a Senate in which all the planets had representatives. As his frustration grew, Anakin found himself turning to Chancellor Palpatine, leader of the Republic. Palpatine seemed to understand exactly how Anakin felt. He was a good listener. Anakin believed that Palpatine was on his side, unlike Obi-Wan.

**Sith Lord**
Palpatine was secretly a Sith Lord, Darth Sidious. He served as Supreme Chancellor of the Republic—but he had plans to destroy it.

Anakin did not realize that Palpatine was secretly trying to destroy the Republic and seize power for himself.

# Unstoppable Feelings

Palpatine's sinister influence increased Anakin's frustration with Obi-Wan and the Jedi Order and left him feeling very confused. When he was chosen to escort Padmé back to Naboo, he finally lost the battle to control his feelings for her.

Padmé was now a Senator and had a
duty to the Republic, but she too could
not prevent herself from falling in love
with Anakin. They were secretly married
on Naboo. Jedi were not supposed to get
emotionally attached to others. Anakin
had broken the rules, but he didn't care.

# Turning to the Dark Side

Anakin had not forgotten his mother Shmi, whom he had left on Tatooine. He began to have terrible nightmares about her, so he went to find her.

**Out of Control**
As he knelt by Shmi's grave, Anakin was angry that he could not save her. He had ignored the Jedi teachings and given into his anger.

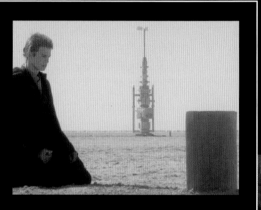

Anakin went back to Tatooine. There he discovered that Shmi had married a farmer named Cliegg Lars, who had freed her from slavery. Anakin also learned that his mother had been kidnapped by Sand People. He went in search of her but he was too late and she died in his arms. Overcome with grief and anger, Anakin took revenge on the Sand People.

## Jedi Hero

Although he was increasingly ruled by his emotions, Anakin had not yet fully turned to the dark side. When the Republic was forced into the Clone Wars, Anakin fought bravely with the Jedi.

The Clone Wars lasted for many years and Anakin and Obi-Wan became famous heroes. Anakin felt truly alive in the heat of the battle and his powers became even stronger.

However, Anakin still felt that he was being held back by the Jedi and that only Palpatine was encouraging his talents. Anakin felt that maybe the Jedi teachings were not right and that greater power lay elsewhere.

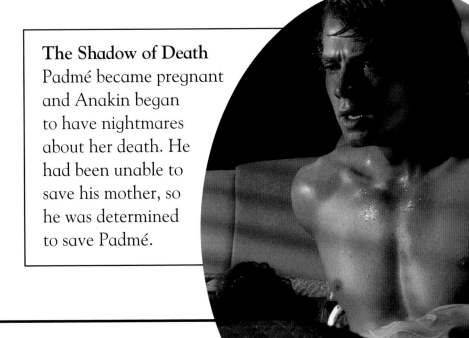

**The Shadow of Death**
Padmé became pregnant and Anakin began to have nightmares about her death. He had been unable to save his mother, so he was determined to save Padmé.

# The Dark Side Wins

Towards the end of the Clone Wars, Palpatine was kidnapped. Anakin and Obi-Wan went to his aid, but it was a trap. Sith Lord Count Dooku was waiting for them. He knocked out Obi-Wan and began to fight Anakin. Palpatine urged Anakin to kill Dooku and Anakin gave in.

A short time later Anakin chose Palpatine over the Jedi and his transition to the dark side was complete. He knelt before Palpatine—his new Sith Master.

*On Palpatine's orders, Anakin led an attack on the Jedi Temple.*

# The End of Anakin

Anakin turned his back on the Jedi and adopted the Sith name Darth Vader. On Palpatine's orders he set out to destroy his former friends and comrades. Darth Vader also became convinced that Padmé and Obi-Wan were plotting against him. He nearly killed his wife and then faced Obi-Wan in an intense lightsaber battle.

Although Darth Vader was driven by anger and the power of the dark side, Obi-Wan won the terrible fight. Vader suffered horrific injuries and burns.

**Anakin the Sith**
When he turned to the dark side, Anakin's eyes turned yellow like all the Sith. He could no longer hide his alliance with evil.

# Rebuilding Darth Vader

Although Darth Vader's body seemed beyond repair, Palpatine refused to give up on his evil apprentice. He took Vader's body to a secret medical facility where it was rebuilt using cyber-technology. Vader needed special breathing equipment and life support systems just to stay alive.

Behind the black armor and a black helmet, it seemed that no part of the human Anakin Skywalker was left. Darth Vader had given himself completely to the ways of the dark side.

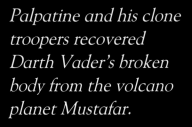

*Palpatine and his clone troopers recovered Darth Vader's broken body from the volcano planet Mustafar.*

# Padmé's Secret

With her husband lost to the dark side, a heartbroken Padmé gave birth to twins, whom she named Luke and Leia. Loyal Jedi Master Obi-Wan Kenobi was by her side, but Padmé had no will to live without Anakin.

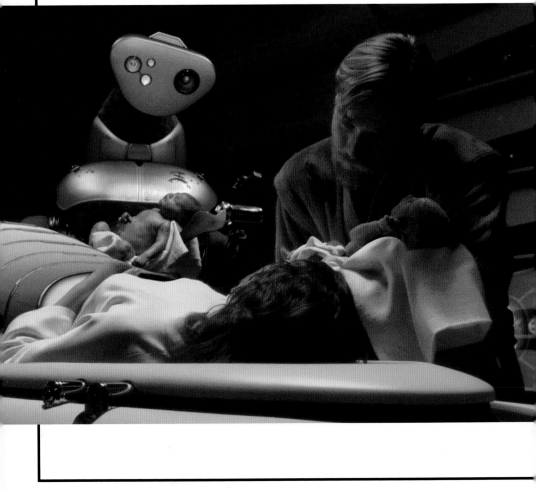

**Reunited**
At first Luke and Leia had no idea that they were twins, but they felt a special connection. When they discovered the truth, they were happy and not completely surprised.

Jedi Master Yoda decided to keep the children a secret from their father. Obi-Wan took Luke to Tatooine to live with Shmi Skywalker's stepson Owen Lars and his wife Beru. Luke's life on the desert planet was hard and lonely. Leia, was taken to the planet Alderaan. She was adopted by Obi-Wan's friend Bail Organa and brought up a princess. Neither twin knew that the other existed. They did not suspect that their father was the feared Sith Lord Vader.

# The Rise of Darth Vader

The Republic had been destroyed and the evil Palpatine ruled the galaxy as Emperor, with Vader by his side. The Sith Lords would let nothing and no one stand in their way. Darth Vader's terrifying appearance, deep voice, and loud artificial breathing struck fear into the hearts of his enemies and allies alike. Even his own generals could not escape Vader's wrath and, as time went by, the Sith's powers grew even stronger.

Anakin Skywalker had been a brave pilot and highly skilled with a lightsaber, but the dark side of the Force continued to corrupt the mind of Darth Vader. He would strangle people without even touching them and he could read the thoughts and feelings of others.

# Civil War

Although the Sith had destroyed the Republic and most of the Jedi, a small group of Rebels bravely opposed the Empire. Known as the Rebel Alliance, they were based on the planet Yavin 4. Little did Darth Vader know that two of the Rebels were his children, Luke and Leia.

The famous Jedi Master Obi-Wan Kenobi faced his former apprentice once again. This time Obi-Wan let Darth Vader win in order to show Luke that, thanks to the Force, a person's spirit continues after death.

**Torture**
When Darth Vader captured the Rebel Princess Leia, he tortured her to learn the Rebels' secrets. He had no idea that she was his own daughter.

# Rebel Victory

The Emperor decided to build a
superweapon known as a Death Star.
It was the size of a small moon and had
the power to blow up entire planets.
However, the Rebels managed to obtain
the plans for the weapon and learned
that it had a fatal flaw.

One exhaust port was
unprotected and if a pilot
fired torpedoes into its shaft, a
chain reaction of explosions would destroy
the whole Death Star. The Rebels sent a
squadron of star fighters and their best
pilot, Luke Skywalker, had one chance to
destroy the Death Star. He did not miss.

# Imperial Fleet

The Rebel Alliance had only a small
number of ships which already bore
the scars of previous battles, but the
Empire had a massive fleet of starships.
The largest and most powerful Imperial
vessels were known as Super Star
Destroyers. Powered by thirteen engines,
the Super Star Destroyers were arrow
shaped and loaded with deadly weapons.

Darth Vader's ship *Executor* was the most powerful Super Star Destroyer. Vader commanded the fleet, but the Emperor gave his orders via hologram.

*Executor*
Vader's magnificent ship led the Imperial fleet into many great battles. It was eventually destroyed by the Rebels.

# Vader's Revenge

When the Rebels blew up the first Death Star, it made Darth Vader and the Emperor extremely angry. They began building a new Death Star and Darth Vader set out to find and destroy the Rebels responsible. Vader sent probe droids to every corner of the galaxy to find the Rebels' new base. He finally located them on the ice planet Hoth.

*Although Darth Vader won the Battle of Hoth, he was not able to destroy the Rebels' best ship, the Millenium Falcon.*

The Sith Lord traveled to Hoth with the Imperial fleet and launched a deadly attack. The Rebels had to evacuate very quickly and their forces were scattered far and wide across the galaxy.

**Luke Skywalker**
After having a vision in which his friends were in danger, Luke Skywalker flew to Cloud City, near the gas planet Bespin. He was now more powerful thanks to the teachings of Jedi Master Yoda.

# Cloud City

Emperor Palpatine had finally told Darth Vader the truth about Luke Skywalker. As Darth Vader laid a trap for Luke on Cloud City, he was looking for more than just a troublesome Rebel— he was searching for his son.

As Luke and Vader fought with lightsabers, Luke still had no idea who lay behind Darth Vader's mask. The fight ended when Vader chopped off Luke's hand. He revealed that he was Luke's father and asked his son to join him and rule the galaxy. Despite his painful wound, Luke was strong with the Force. He refused to turn to the dark side.

# Vader's Choice

For many years, Darth Vader had been loyal to Emperor Palpatine. However, meeting his son Luke—a good and true person—seemed to change him. Could it be that some part of Anakin Skywalker remained behind Vader's mask?

Palpatine had predicted that Luke would come to them and he would be turned to the dark side. When Luke surrendered, it seemed that Palpatine would be proved right. As father and son fought once more, Luke felt anger and hatred and drew close to the dark side. At the last moment Luke was able to control his feelings and refused to join the dark side. As an enraged Palpatine attacked Luke, Anakin Skywalker finally returned from the dark side to save his son.

**Death of an Emperor**
As Palpatine tortured Luke with deadly Force lightning, Darth Vader could not bear to watch. He picked up his Master and threw him down a bottomless reactor shaft. The Emperor was dead!

# The Death of Darth Vader

At the vital moment, Darth Vader returned from his nightmare. Luke had reminded him that he was once a great Jedi named Anakin Skywalker. However, as Vader saved his son, he was fatally wounded by the Emperor.

As Anakin lay dying, he asked Luke to remove his helmet so that he could look at his son's face with his own eyes. When Anakin died, his body disappeared into the light side of the Force. Luke was sad that his father was dead but proud of him too. The light side of the Force had overcome the dark side and Anakin Skywalker had returned.

On the forest moon of Endor, Luke burned Vader's armor. All around the galaxy, everyone celebrated the end of Palpatine and his evil Empire.

**Jedi Restored**
After his death, Anakin took his place with the other great Jedi heroes Yoda and Obi-Wan Kenobi.

# THE LEGENDARY
# YODA

Written by
Catherine Saunders

# The greatest Jedi

This is Yoda, defender of the galaxy, Master of the Force, and the greatest Jedi who has ever lived. How exactly did he become such a legendary Jedi?

Yoda is nearly 900 years old, but very little is known about his early life. He is from a remote planet, but which one is a mystery. Amazingly, Yoda did not know that he had Force powers until he was an adult. His path toward the Jedi began when he left his home to find work.

**Galactic heroes**
The Jedi believe in peace and justice. They use the light side of the Force. Their enemies are the Sith.

Yoda's ship crashed on a strange planet, and there he met a mysterious Jedi Master who sensed his potential. The Jedi Master invited Yoda to become his apprentice, known as a Padawan.

Three fingers

Green skin

Jedi robe

Walking cane

Yoda carries a cane, known as a gimer stick. It helps him to walk, but when chewed it can be a source of food or pain relief.

# Respected Jedi

As time passed, Yoda proved himself to be a skilled Jedi. When he had completed his Padawan training, he became a Jedi Knight, which meant he could go on important missions. By the age of 96 he had become a Jedi Master. Later, Yoda was elected to join the Jedi High Council.

Finally, Yoda
became the
Grand Master,
or leader, of the
whole Jedi Order.

*Jedi Master Mace Windu is head of the Jedi High Council.*

Grand Master Yoda is respected
throughout the galaxy. He is famous
for his wisdom and his knowledge
of the Force.

*The Jedi High Council is a
group of 12 wise Jedi who
guide the Order and advise
the leaders of the galaxy.*

# Force powers

Every Jedi is trained in the ways of the Force, the invisible energy that surrounds all living things. This powerful energy has a light side, which can be used for good, and a dark side, which can be used for evil. Yoda's ability to use the Force is greater than that of any other Jedi.

*Yoda can use the Force to deflect the Sith's deadliest weapon—Force lightning.*

Yoda has spent many years studying the Force and wields its powers wisely. He uses it to guide his

*Yoda meditates using the Force.*

actions and decisions, yet, if necessary, he can also harness the power of the Force. Yoda can use the Force to leap great distances, lift heavy objects, and control the minds of others.

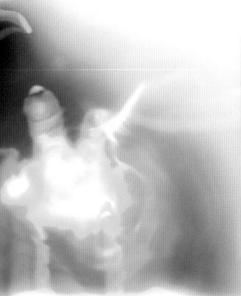

*Yoda can use the Force to lift huge rocks. He uses the Force to throw them, too.*

# Size matters not

Yoda is only 66 cm (2 feet 2 inches) tall, but he is a fierce fighter. The Jedi's preferred weapon is a lightsaber and Yoda is a famous swordmaster.

*There are seven main forms of lightsaber combat. Yoda's favorite style is Form IV, known as Ataru.*

*Lightsaber*

*Determined expression*

*Tiny feet*

*Yoda needs all his lightsaber skills when he duels Darth Sidious.*
*He has met his match in the powerful Sith Lord.*

What Yoda lacks in size he makes up for in athletic ability. He uses quick jumps, twists, and turns to confuse his opponents, and draws strength from the light side of the Force. Like all Jedi, however, Yoda enters into battle only when there is no other option.

Power cell
in handle

Blade appears
here

*Every Jedi builds his own lightsaber. Yoda's fits into his small hands perfectly.*

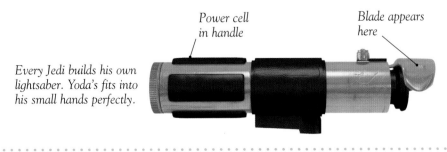

# Wise teacher

*Most Jedi Masters train only one Padawan apprentice at a time, but Yoda has many Jedi pupils.*

Over the years, many Jedi have been trained by the legendary Master Yoda, including Count Dooku and Ki-Adi-Mundi. No one knows more about being a Jedi, but Yoda is a tough teacher. He expects his pupils to work very hard.

*Ornate cloak*

*Red Sith lightsaber*

*Count Dooku was a difficult student. He had lots of unconventional ideas about being a Jedi.*

106

Yoda taught Count
Dooku and Ki-Adi-
Mundi how to fight with
lightsabers and how to
uphold peace and justice
in the galaxy. He also
instructed them in
the ways of the light
side of the Force.

Both Dooku and
Ki-Adi-Mundi became
skilled Jedi Knights,
and later Masters.
However, Dooku was
not happy with life as a
Jedi and left the Order.
Count Dooku's current
whereabouts and
occupation are unknown.

Lightsaber

Boots

Ki-Adi-Mundi was
a dedicated pupil and
he is now a brave
Jedi Master.

# Preparing future Jedi

One of Yoda's most important jobs is selecting the new recruits to the Jedi Order. These recruits are known as younglings. They are sensitive to the Force, but don't know how to use their powers yet. Yoda decides who has the potential to become a Jedi.

Yoda enjoys passing on his years of knowledge to the younglings. He is a wise and patient teacher. He is also very funny! The younglings enjoy being taught by the legendary Jedi.

*The younglings live and train in the Jedi Temple on Coruscant.*

*Jedi Master Qui-Gon Jinn believes that young Anakin Skywalker is the Chosen One—a great Jedi who will bring balance to the Force.*

# Strong opinions

Yoda's great age and his knowledge of the Force give him great insight into the thoughts and feelings of others. He uses his wisdom and experience to guide the Jedi Council when they are faced with difficult decisions.

Jedi Qui-Gon Jinn wants Anakin Skywalker to become a Jedi, too, but Yoda does not think it is a good idea. The boy has strong Force powers, but Anakin is too old to begin training. Yoda also senses much fear in him and advises the Jedi Council to refuse Qui-Gon's request.

*Soon after, Qui-Gon is destroyed by the Sith Darth Maul. His dying wish is for Obi-Wan to train Anakin, so Yoda changes his mind.*

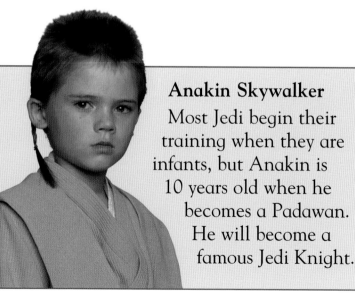

**Anakin Skywalker**
Most Jedi begin their training when they are infants, but Anakin is 10 years old when he becomes a Padawan. He will become a famous Jedi Knight.

# Wise Yoda

Master Yoda is famous for his
wisdom. Many important people
visit him if they need advice or are
looking for information. When
Obi-Wan Kenobi needs to locate
a planet that has mysteriously
disappeared from the Jedi Archives,
he turns to Yoda. Sure enough,
Yoda finds the answer.

*Yoda tells Obi-Wan that a Jedi must have erased the planet from
the Jedi Archives, but who it was or why they did it is a mystery.*

*Anakin dreams that his pregnant wife, Padmé, will die in childbirth.*
*He will do anything to make sure that doesn't happen.*

Anakin Skywalker has nightmares that his wife, Padmé, will die, so he asks Master Yoda for advice. Yoda warns the Jedi that fear of loss will lead him to the dark side. Sadly, Anakin doesn't listen to Yoda.

### Kamino

Obi-Wan is searching for the planet Kamino. When he locates it, he finds a huge clone army there.

The Jedi go to Geonosis to rescue Padmé, Anakin, and Obi-Wan.

# Yoda to the rescue

The Jedi believe in peace, freedom, and diplomacy, but sometimes conflict is the only option. Trouble has been growing in the galaxy for some time, because a group known as the Separatists want to break away from the democratic rule of the Republic.

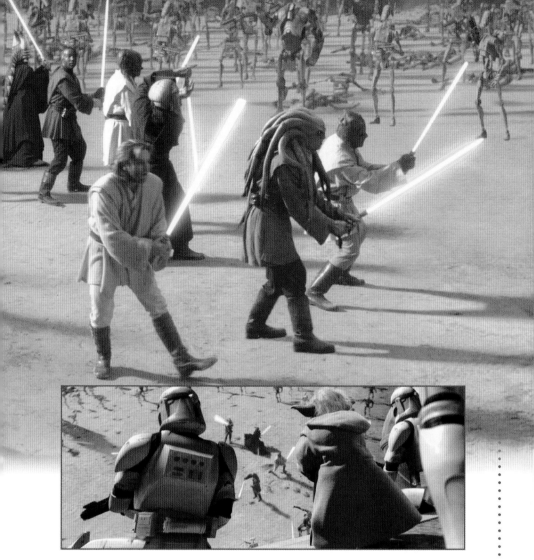

*Yoda arrives with soldiers from the Clone Army Obi-Wan discovered on Kamino.*

On Geonosis, the Jedi find themselves surrounded by the Separatists' huge Droid Army. Things look serious—until Master Yoda arrives with reinforcements.

# Epic duel

On Geonosis, Yoda meets an old friend—Count Dooku. However, Dooku is now a Separatist leader, and therefore an enemy of the Jedi.

Anakin Skywalker and Obi-Wan Kenobi duel Dooku, but he is too powerful. It is up to Yoda to defeat him. As the Jedi and his former Padawan duel, Dooku uses Force lightning. Yoda knows that only a Sith would do that. He realizes that Dooku has turned to the dark side.

## Sith Lord

Dooku's Sith Master is Darth Sidious. Sidious has a secret identity— he is also the leader of the Republic, Supreme Chancellor Palpatine.

# High General Yoda

The events on Geonosis are the start of an epic galactic conflict called the Clone Wars. The Clone Army becomes the Grand Army of the Republic and fights the Separatist Droid Army in many battles.

The Clone Army is led by High General Yoda. The other Jedi also become generals and bravely fight to save the galaxy from the Separatists.

During the Clone Wars, Yoda's reputation as a great Jedi warrior grows. At the Battle of Rugosa, he defeats a battalion of battle droids with only a few clones to help him!

**Clone Army**
Every clone trooper is a copy, or clone, of a bounty hunter named Jango Fett. That means they all look the same. The clones are skilled and obedient fighters.

# Elected leader

Yoda is the elected leader of the Jedi Council during the Clone Wars. He is now the Grand Master and Master of the Order—the oldest, wisest, and most important Jedi. Yoda's job is to guide and protect the Republic.

*Sometimes Jedi, such as Ki-Adi-Mundi, attend Jedi Council meetings via hologram.*

Although Yoda undertakes some important frontline missions in the Clone Wars, he also directs many battles from the Jedi Temple in Coruscant. Yoda uses his wisdom to advise the Jedi Council and to plan the Clone Army's battle tactics. The Jedi are strong fighters, but Master Yoda wants to restore peace to the galaxy as soon as possible.

# Turning point

For three years, the Clone Wars rage throughout the galaxy. Many battles are fought and many lives are lost. Master Yoda senses that a Sith Lord is secretly controlling events and he is determined to find him.

Yoda must also help his old friends, the Wookiees. Their forest planet, Kashyyyk, is about to be invaded by the Separatist Droid Army, so Yoda and the Republic forces arrive to help defend it.

*Clone Commander Gree, Yoda, and Chewbacca discuss their battle plans.*

**Wookiee friends**
Tarfful is a wise leader and Chewbacca is a brave warrior. Later, Master Yoda will need their help, too.

However, neither the Republic nor the Separatists will win the Battle of Kashyyyk. Something far worse is about to happen...

# Order 66

Darth Sidious gives Order 66 via hologram.

Yoda senses that a mysterious Sith is becoming very powerful, but he does not know who it is, or what he is planning. Suddenly, the truth is revealed. The clone troopers receive secret Order 66 from Darth Sidious—it tells them to turn on their Jedi generals!

Throughout the galaxy, the Clone Army turns against its allies and many brave Jedi are slaughtered. On Kashyyyk, Master Yoda is in grave danger.

Yoda senses a major disturbance in the Force: Anakin Skywalker has given in to the dark side and become the Sith lord, Darth Vader.

Fortunately, Yoda's Force powers do not let him down. He destroys the clone troopers before they can attack him. Yoda must now think quickly to save the galaxy...

*Yoda has no choice. He must attack his clone troopers, or they will attack him.*

# Jedi vs. Sith

Yoda returns to the Jedi Temple on Coruscant and learns the terrible truth: Chancellor Palpatine is the Sith Lord Darth Sidious. Worse still, nearly all the Jedi have been murdered, including the younglings. Yoda has no choice— he must confront Darth Sidious.

*Yoda clings on to a Senatorial pod. The epic duel has drained his strength.*

Sith Lord and Jedi Master are well-matched. Both are experts in lightsaber combat and Masters of the Force. Sidious is determined to prove the power of the dark side by defeating the legendary Jedi. After a duel that destroys much of the Senate, Sidious seems to have won the battle. Yoda, however, takes a secret way out. The Force has shown him what he must do, so the Jedi Master escapes.

*Yoda and Darth Sidious duel inside the Galactic Senate.*

# Yoda's sadness

Yoda escapes from Coruscant with the help of Senator Bail Organa. They travel to Polis Massa, a remote outpost on an asteroid, where they will be safe. He has survived his duel with Darth Sidious, but Yoda is filled with sadness. Many brave Jedi have fallen, and Anakin Skywalker has turned to the dark side. Yoda deeply regrets that he did not realize Chancellor Palpatine's true identity.

*Once again, Obi-Wan Kenobi needs Yoda's wisdom.*

**Brave Senator**
Bail Organa is from the planet Alderaan. He is a loyal friend to the Jedi and a trusted Senator.

On Polis Massa, Yoda is faced with another big problem: Obi-Wan has rescued Anakin's wife, Padmé, and she is due to give birth to twins.

# Protecting the future

Padmé gives birth to healthy twins, Luke and Leia, but she doesn't survive their birth. Yoda senses that the twins have strong Force powers, which means they could become great Jedi. If their Sith father finds out about them, however, he will surely want them for the dark side! So Yoda comes up with a plan to hide Luke and Leia from Darth Vader.

*Yoda consults with Obi-Wan Kenobi and Bail Organa. They must find a way to keep Luke and Leia safe.*

*Obi-Wan gives baby Luke to his father Anakin Skywalker's stepfamily, Beru and Owen Lars.*

Obi-Wan will take Luke to Tatooine, while Bail Organa will adopt Leia and raise her on Alderaan. Their father will not know of their existence. Meanwhile, Sidious is still determined to complete Order 66 and destroy the entire Jedi Order. Master Yoda must hide.

*Bail Organa and his wife, Breha, have always longed for a child of their own.*

# Into exile

A dark time for the galaxy has begun. Most Jedi are dead or, like Yoda, in hiding. The Republic is no more and Darth Sidious has declared that he is the ruler of the Galactic Empire. As Emperor Palpatine, he will rule using fear and the power of the dark side.

*Yoda chooses Dagobah as a refuge because it is remote and uninhabited. The Sith will not find him here.*

*Yoda builds himself a hut made of mud and parts of the ship that brought him to Dagobah.*

Grand Master Yoda hides to protect himself, and also to ensure that the Jedi Order is not completely destroyed. He chooses the remote, swampy planet of Dagobah in the Outer Rim of the galaxy.

Yoda will be safe from the Sith on Dagobah. The Force has shown him that better times are to come, but it will be many years before the galaxy sees any signs of hope.

# A new pupil

Yoda spends more than 20 years in exile on Dagobah. During that time, the Empire grows more powerful—and more terrible. The people of the galaxy live in growing fear.

Only a brave few dare to fight against Emperor Palpatine. These people are known as the Rebel Alliance. X-wing pilot Luke Skywalker is one of the rebels. He travels to Dagobah to find Yoda and ask him to train him to be a Jedi.

*The spirit of Obi-Wan Kenobi tells Luke that he will find Yoda on Dagobah.*

**Future Jedi**
Luke Skywalker is
the son of Anakin
Skywalker. He is a
brave rebel and has
strong Force powers.

When Luke meets a small, green
alien, however, he doesn't realize that
he is the legendary Jedi Master!
He asks him to take him to meet
Yoda. Luke has much to learn...

# Jedi in training

Yoda senses that Luke Skywalker has enormous potential, but he also senses the same fear in him that led his father to the dark side. Yoda agrees to train the rebel pilot.

The training is hard. Yoda is tough on Luke because he wants to prepare him for the challenges that lie ahead. He teaches Luke how to feel and use the Force, but warns him of the power of the dark side. Luke chooses to leave Dagobah before his training is complete, but he promises to return soon.

*Luke wants to save his friends from Vader, but Yoda thinks he should complete his training.*

# Not the end

Luke keeps his promise to Yoda and returns to Dagobah to finish his Jedi training. By this time, however, Master Yoda is sick and tells Luke that he does not have long to live.

*As promised, Luke returns to Dagobah. Much has happened since he left Master Yoda. In his first duel with Darth Vader, Luke lost his right hand.*

Yoda's wisdom and knowledge of the Force show him that death is simply part of nature. He does not fear it. Before he passes, Yoda tells Luke that his training is complete—he is a Jedi. But Luke's final test will be to face Darth Vader, his father, once again. As his life fades, Yoda also reveals a secret that he has kept safe for more than 20 years—there is another Skywalker. Luke has a twin sister named Leia.

# Yoda's legacy

For nearly 900 years, Yoda helped to guide the Jedi Order. He went on many dangerous missions, fought bravely in many battles, and used his wisdom to help the galaxy. He was respected by those who value peace, justice, and freedom, and feared by those who use the dark side of the Force.

*At the end of his life, Anakin Skywalker finally finds his way back to the light side of the Force.*

Yoda did not live to see the Sith defeated, but for a legendary Jedi death is not the end. Yoda's Force powers are so strong that his spirit becomes one with the Force.

Like Obi-Wan Kenobi and Anakin Skywalker, Yoda will live on through the Force. As Luke Skywalker builds a new Jedi Order, Yoda will be there to guide him.

# Glossary

**Apprentice**
A person who is learning a skill.

**Assassin**
Someone who is hired to kill somebody.

**Bounty hunter**
Someone who searches for and captures people for a reward.

**Chancellor**
The person who leads the government, known as the Senate.

**Coruscant**
One of the most important planets in the galaxy.

**Dark side**
The part of the Force associated with fear and hatred.

**Droid**
A kind of robot.

**Duel**
A battle between two people.

**Emperor**
The leader of an Empire is called an Emperor. Palpatine is the Emperor who rules the Galactic Empire.

**Force**
The energy created by all living things.

**Force lightning**
Deadly rays of blue energy used by the Sith.

**Galactic Empire**
A group of worlds ruled over by one unelected leader, known as the Emperor.

**Galaxy**
A group of millions of stars and planets.

**Grand Master**
The head of the Jedi Order.

**Jedi**
A being who has the power to use the light side of the Force.

**Jedi Archives**
A collection of thousands of years of knowledge, stored in the Jedi Temple.

**Jedi Council**
An organized group of Jedi and Jedi Masters who govern the Jedi academies, temples, and other organizations.

**Jedi Knight**
A warrior with special powers who defends the good of the galaxy.

**Jedi Master**
A rank for Jedi Knights who have performed an exceptional deed, serve on the Jedi Council, or have helped a Padawan pass the Jedi Trials.

**Jedi Order**
A group of beings who defend peace and justice in the galaxy.

**Jedi Temple**
The headquarters of the Jedi Order, located on the planet of Coruscant.

**Kaminoans**
The tall, thin species that lives on the planet Kamino.

**Lightsaber**
A Jedi's and Sith's weapon. It has a sword-like blade of pure energy.

**Light Side**
The part of the Force associated with goodness, compassion, and healing

**Master of the Order**
The elected leader of the Jedi Council.

**Outer Rim**
The most remote part of the known galaxy.

**Rebel Alliance**
A group of people who want to remove the Emperor from power.

**Republic**
A world or group of worlds in which people vote for their leaders.

**Padawan**
A youngling who is chosen to serve an apprenticeship with a Jedi Knight or Master.

**Senate**
The governing body of the Republic.

**Separatists**
A group of people who want to separate themselves from the Galactic Republic.

**Sith**
Enemies of the Jedi who use the dark side of the Force.

**Slave**
A person who is owned by another person.

**Starfighter**
A small, fast spaceship used by Jedi and others.

**Trade Federation**
A group of merchants and transporters who control the movement of goods in the galaxy.

**X-wing**
A rebel starfighter whose four wings are arranged in an "X" shape.

**Youngling**
A Force-sensitive child who is training to become a Jedi.

# Index

Alderaan 41, 43, 44, 79, 129, 131
Amidala, Padmé 10, 12, 15, 17, 18, 22, 23, 24, 40, 59, 63, 66, 67, 71, 74, 78, 113, 114, 129, 130
apprentice 53, 58, 59, 60, 82
Ataru 104

battle droids 119
Battle of Kashyyyk 123
Battle of Rugosa 119
Bespin 89
Binks, Jar Jar  10

C-3PO 44, 54
Chewbacca  44, 122-123
Chosen One 110
Clone Army 113, 115, 118-119, 121, 124
clone troopers 76, 119, 124, 125
Clone Wars 70, 72, 118-119, 120, 121, 122, 123
Cloud City 89, 90
Commander Cody 29
Commander Gree 122
Coruscant 6, 10, 11, 19, 31, 35, 60, 109, 121, 126, 128
Count Dooku 22, 23, 24, 25, 26, 27, 30, 31, 106, 107, 116-117

Dagobah 132, 133, 134, 135, 137, 138, 139
dark side 13, 72, 73, 75, 78, 81, 91, 93, 95, 102, 113, 116, 124,
127, 128, 130, 137, 140
Darth Maul 12, 13, 14, 111
Darth Sidious 33, 42, 65, 105, 117, 124, 126, 127, 128, 131, 132 (see Palpatine)
Darth Tyrannus 22
Darth Vader 33, 36, 38, 39, 42, 45, 46, 47, 48, 53, 74, 75, 76, 78, 81, 82, 83, 87, 88, 89, 90, 91, 92, 93, 94, 124, 130, 139 (see Anakin Skywalker)
Death Star 43, 44, 45, 48, 84, 85, 89
Dooku, Count 63, 72
droids 54, 59, 88
Droid Army 115, 118, 122
duel 116-117, 126-127

Emperor 53, 81, 84, 87, 88, 93, 94

Fett, Boba  20
Fett, Jango 19, 20, 21, 119
Force 9, 13, 15, 26, 38, 39, 47, 48, 49, 53, 56, 57, 60, 61, 81, 82, 91, 93, 95, 98, 101, 102-103, 105, 107, 108, 110, 111, 124, 125, 127, 130, 133, 135, 139, 140, 141
Force lightning 102, 116

Galactic Empire 132, 134

galaxy 6, 10, 18, 33, 38, 40, 41, 48, 53, 64, 89, 91, 95
General Grievous  30, 33, 34, 35
generals 81
Geonosis 21, 22, 23, 24, 25, 28, 114-115, 118
gimer stick 99
Grand Army of the Republic 118
Grand Master 101, 120

hologram 120
Hoth 88, 89

Invisible Hand  31

Jedi 53, 56, 57, 59, 60, 61, 63, 67, 68, 70, 71, 73, 74, 78, 82, 89, 90, 91, 92, 94, 95
Jedi Archives 112
Jedi Council 11, 13, 19, 22, 29, 58, 59, 100, 101, 120, 121
Jedi Knight 6, 8, 9, 14, 25, 53, 60, 63
Jedi Master 82, 89
Jedi Order 66
Jedi Temple 36, 60, 73, 91, 109, 111, 121, 126
Jinn, Qui-Gon 7, 10, 11, 12, 13, 14, 56, 57, 58, 59, 110, 111

Kamino  18, 113, 115
Kashyyyk 122-123, 124
Kenobi, Obi-Wan 6, 8, 9, 10, 11, 12, 13, 14, 15, 16, 17, 18, 19, 20, 21, 22, 23, 24, 25, 26,

# Index

27, 28, 29, 30, 31, 32, 33, 34, 35, 36, 37, 38, 39, 40, 41, 42, 43, 44, 45, 46, 47, 48, 49, 42, 56, 58, 59, 61, 63, 64, 66, 71, 72, 74, 75, 78, 79, 82, 95, 110, 111, 112, 113, 114, 116, 128, 129, 130, 131, 134, 141

Ki-Adi-Mundi 106, 107, 120

Lars, Beru 41, 79, 131
Lars, Cliegg 69
Lars, Owen 6, 41, 79, 131
lightsaber 13, 34, 39, 46, 47, 74, 81, 91, 104-105, 106, 107, 127
light side 98, 102, 140

Master of the Order 101, 127
meditation 103
Millenium Falcon 44, 45, 89
Mustafar 38, 76

Naboo 8, 16, 59, 66, 67

Order 66 36, 37, 124-125, 131
Organa, Bail 79, 128, 129, 130, 131
Organa, Breha 131
Outer Rim 133

Padawan 6, 8, 12, 14, 15, 26, 32, 37, 61, 63, 99, 100, 106, 111, 118

Palapatine 30, 31, 32, 33, 37, 39, 40, 41, 42, 53, 64, 65, 66, 71, 72, 73, 74, 76, 81, 90, 92, 93, 95, 117, 126, 128, 132, 134 (see Darth Sidious)
planets 54, 56, 57, 58, 60, 64, 76, 79, 82, 84, 88, 89, 90
Podrace 57
Princess Leia 41, 43, 44, 46, 47, 48, 79, 82, 83, 130, 131, 139
Polis Massa 128, 129

R2-D2 43
Rebel Alliance 82, 86, 135
Rebels 82, 83, 84, 85, 87, 88, 89, 90, 134, 135, 137
Republic 64, 65, 67, 70, 81, 82, 114, 117, 122, 123

Sand People 69
Senate 64, 126, 127
Senator 64, 67, 128, 129
Separatists 114, 115, 116, 118, 122, 123
Shmi 54, 68, 69, 79
Sifo-Dyas 18
Sith 53, 61, 63, 65, 72, 73, 74, 75, 81, 82, 89, 98, 102, 105, 106, 116, 117, 122, 124, 126, 127, 130, 132, 133
Skywalker, Anakin 11, 14, 15, 16, 17, 23, 24, 26, 27, 28, 30, 31, 32,

33, 37, 39, 40, 41, 49, 53, 54, 56, 57, 58, 59, 60, 61, 63, 64, 65, 66, 67, 68, 69, 70, 71, 72, 73, 74, 75, 76, 78, 81, 92, 93, 94, 95, 110, 111, 113, 114, 116, 124, 128 (see Darth Vader)
Skywalker, Luke 41, 42, 43, 46, 47, 48, 79, 82, 85, 89, 90, 91, 92, 93, 94, 95, 130, 131, 134, 135, 137, 138, 139, 141
Slave I 20
Solo, Han 44, 46, 47
Stewjon 6
Super Star Destroyers 86, 87

Tarfful 123
Tatooine 11, 12, 41, 42, 54, 56, 57, 58, 68, 69, 79, 131
teacher 106-107, 108-109, 137
Theed 11
Trade Federation 10, 11, 12, 59

Utapau 34, 35, 36

Wessell, Zam 17
Windu, Mace 24, 101
wisdom 106-107, 112-113, 120-121, 128
Wookiee 44, 122-123

X-wing 134